Clifford THE BIG RED DOG®
Clifford Makes a Splash

by Quinlan B. Lee
Illustrated by Steve Haefele

Based on the Scholastic book series
"Clifford The Big Red Dog"
by Norman Bridwell

ISBN-13: 978-0-545-00021-5
ISBN-10: 0-545-00021-1

Designed by Michael Massen

12 11 10 9 8 7 6 5 4 3   9 10 11/0

Printed in the U.S.A.
First printing, May 2007

SCHOLASTIC INC.

New York   Toronto   London   Auckland   Sydney
Mexico City   New Delhi   Hong Kong   Buenos Aires

It was the hottest day of the summer.
Nothing could cool Clifford off. Not even
the fan Emily Elizabeth gave him.

"Ready or not, here I come!" Cleo yelled.

Splash!

"Clifford, check out Cleo's new puppy pool!" T-Bone said. "Isn't it cool?"

"It sure *looks* cool," Clifford said. "And small."

Cleo sighed. "I'm sorry, big guy," she said.

Clifford went to the Birdwell Island pool
with Emily Elizabeth.

"Would you like to hop in and cool off?" she asked.

Woof, woof!

"Watch out, everyone, here comes Clifford," said Emily Elizabeth.

Clifford was ready to make a splash.

One, two, three . . .

SPLASH!

When Clifford jumped in, all the water splashed out!

"Sorry, boy, you're just too big for the pool," said Emily Elizabeth sadly.

Clifford needed a place to cool off that
was big and had lots and lots of water.

Where could he go?

The beach! It was the perfect place for a
Big Red Dog to cool off in a big way.

Clifford ran into the water.

Splish, splish, SPLASH!

"Surf's up!" Charley called.

"Watch out!" cried Charley's dad.

Clifford was sorry he had soaked everyone at the beach.

"I guess you'd better head home, boy," said Charley.

At home, Emily Elizabeth's mother was watering her garden.

She pointed the hose at Clifford.

"Is that better?" she asked.

Woof, woof!

It felt great!

"Are you having fun without us?"
Cleo asked.

"Not anymore," said Clifford.

"Come on!"

Emily Elizabeth and her friends came home
and joined in the fun.

"Clifford looks like he finally cooled off,"
said Charley.

"Of course," said Emily Elizabeth. "Any place Clifford goes is always the coolest place to be."

Do You Remember?

Circle the right answer.

1. Why can't Clifford play in Cleo's puppy pool?
   a. The weather is too hot.
   b. He is too big.
   c. He would rather sit in his doghouse.

2. Why does Clifford go to the beach?
   a. Because he wants to sunbathe.
   b. He wants to visit Emily Elizabeth.
   c. To cool off.

Which happened first?

Which happened next?

Which happened last?

Write a 1, 2, or 3 in the space after each sentence.

Clifford goes to the pool. _____

Clifford soaks everyone at the beach. _____

Cleo and T-Bone play in the puppy pool. _____